Published in 2015 by Simply Read Books www.simplyreadbooks.com
Text © 2015 Jennifer Lloyd
Illustrations © 2015 Jacqui Lee

Library and Archives Canada Cataloguing in Publication
Lloyd, Jennifer, author
Taffy time / written by Jennifer Lloyd;
illustrated by Jacqui Lee.

ISBN 978-1-927018-62-0 (bound)

I. Lee, Jacqui, illustrator II. Title.

PS8623.L69T34 2015   jC813'.6   C2014-905984-1

We gratefully acknowledge for their financial support of our publishing
program the Canada Council for the Arts, the BC Arts Council, and the
Government of Canada through the Canada Book Fund (CBF).

Manufactured in Malaysia

Book design by Naomi MacDougall

10 9 8 7 6 5 4 3 2 1

Taffy Time

JENNIFER LLOYD

ILLUSTRATED BY JACQUI LEE

SIMPLY READ BOOKS

It's spring at Sugar Hill Farm.

Time to make maple syrup.

"I want to go to the sugar shack too!" Kate cries.

"Hmm . . ." Dad hesitates.

"Please!"

"Okay. But you have to let
Audrey and I do our work."

Kate tugs the zipper of her fuzzy
jacket. She tugs harder.
"My zipper is stuck!"

"Soon you will be old enough
to work zippers every time,"
says Mom.

At last Kate is ready.
She bursts out the door.

"Wait!" Mom calls her back.
"I forgot to give your dad
these. Don't lose them."

Kate tucks the popsicle sticks safely in her pocket. She hurries to catch up by stepping into her sister's snow prints.

Passing the barn, the three make
their way towards the sugar shack.

"Look—a robin!" shouts Kate.

Soon they come to a tiny stream. Audrey jumps easily to the other side.

Kate leaps...

SPLASH

Dad comes to the rescue.

At last they reach a grove of trees with tin pails attached to them.

"What is that noise?" asks Kate.

"The sounds are coming from the sugar maples," Audrey explains. "The liquid dripping into the pails is tree sap."

"The pails are full. We must empty them into the holding tank," says Dad.

Kate dips her fingers into
some sap.

"Mmm. It's sweet."

She tries to
lift a pail off the tree, but . . .

Dad groans. "Audrey and
I will do this part."

Kate makes snow angels while her
father and sister lug pails back and
forth.

When all the buckets are emptied,
she follows Audrey into the shack.

"What's happening now?" Kate asks.

"The sap is going into the evaporator," answers Dad. "The evaporator warms the sap and boils the water out of it so that it can turn into sticky syrup."

Kate watches the swirling sap. From time to time, Audrey checks the temperature. Kate pretends to read the thermometer too.

The sap keeps bubbling, slowly growing golden.

"Is it ready yet?"
Kate asks Dad.

"Patience," says Dad.
"Making maple syrup
takes a long time."

The fire beneath the evaporator
makes the room warm and cozy.
Kate takes off a mitten and waves it
in the rising steam clouds.

"Don't!" cries Dad.

Oops! The mitten lands in the sap. Dad fishes it out.

Kate sighs.

Dad needs to keep the fire going. He chops
wood and carries it into the sugar shack.

Kate tries to pick up a piece. It is too heavy.

A twig pokes out from under
the snow. Kate yanks on it but
it is frozen to the ground.

She searches for more twigs.
A baby chipmunk scurries past.
Kate follows its trail.

A family of geese honk at her as
they fly overhead.

She continues to explore until…

looking back, she can't see
the sugar shack anymore.

Kate is tired and hungry.
The forest seems very still.

"Dad!" she cries.

Dad hears her faint cry and comes running. "Kate! Why did you wander away?"

"I was looking for twigs for the fire. I just wanted to help," she explains.

"There is something you could do . . . if only I hadn't forgotten the popsicle sticks."

Suddenly Kate remembers.

"I have them! Mom gave them to me."

"Great," says Dad.

Back at the shack, Dad fetches
a jug of hot syrup.

"First, pour the syrup onto the
snow," Dad instructs Kate.
"Then you wind the stick around."

"I can do it," Kate says.
And she does.

"For you!" she says to Dad. "And you too," she says to Audrey.

"Thank you," they answer, smiling.

Soon Mom arrives with lunch.

Together, the family celebrates
with a picnic of soup, sandwiches
and delicious maple taffy.